Pups the Turbots

Bath · New York · Cologne · Melbourne · Delhi
Hong Kong · Shenzhen · Singapore

Ryder and the PAW Patrol are playing volleyball on the beach.

"Get the ball!" bark Zuma and Rubble.

The pups are soon joined by Captain Turbot and his friend.

"Hi, everyone," says Captain Turbot. "This is my cousin, François, from France."

"Ooh-la-la!" says François. "The only thing better than football is volleyball. Make room for one more!"

Captain Turbot leaves François behind.

"I think I saw a blue-footed booby bird down by the bay," says Captain Turbot. "If I can get a picture, it might make the cover of *Marine Bird Monthly*!"

"Good luck," calls Ryder.

Captain Turbot heads off in his boat. When he looks through his binoculars he sees François kitesurfing.

"I hope François's fancy footwork doesn't scare my bird away," Captain Turbot says to himself.

Wally the walrus pops up and barks loudly. At first Captain Turbot doesn't understand but when he looks up at where Wally is pointing, he sees the blue-footed booby bird.

"There it is!" gasps Captain Turbot. "On my boat!"

Captain Turbot is so busy trying to take a photograph he falls overboard and scares the booby bird.

"Oh no! Come back!" cries Captain Turbot as the bird flies away.

Ryder and the pups are still playing on the beach when Wally swims up.

"Hi, Wally," says Ryder. "What's wrong?

Wally barks, points and flaps his flippers until Ryder understands the problem.

"It's Captain Turbot!" says Ryder. "He found his bird, but lost his boat... I think Wally is trying to tell us that the captain needs our help!"

Ryder pulls out his PupPad. "No job is too big, no pup is too small. PAW Patrol to the Lookout!"

At the Lookout, the pups are ready for action.

"Pups, Captain Turbot needs us," says Ryder. "He was trying to take a photo of the blue-footed booby bird but ended up in the bay."

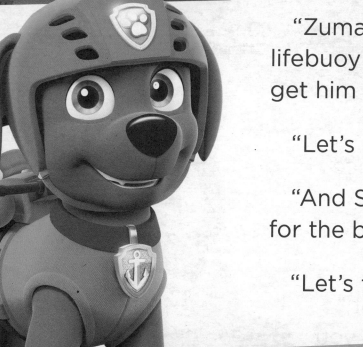

"Zuma, I need you to use your lifebuoy to rescue the captain and get him back to his boat."

"Let's dive in!" says Zuma.

"And Skye, I need you to search for the bird's nest from above."

"Let's take to the sky!" she says.

Ryder, Zuma and Skye race across the bay.

"There he is!" cries Zuma.

"Hang on, Captain Turbot," calls Ryder. "Zuma will get you – I'll get your boat."

Zuma launches the lifebuoy and it lands right over Captain Turbot. Zuma pulls him back to his boat.

"Woo-hoo! Thanks, Zuma," he says.

Zuma and Captain Turbot climb aboard the Flounder. Ryder and Skye are already there waiting.

"We'll help you get some pictures of the booby bird," says Ryder.

"Thank you," says Captain Turbot.

Suddenly, François surfs in, almost knocking over his cousin.

"OK, Horatio. I will take a picture of this bird for you."

Captain Turbot sighs.

Meanwhile, Skye is flying across the bay looking for the blue-footed booby bird. She spots its nest on the cliff top.

"That's it!" Skye shouts into her helmet mike. "I couldn't miss those bright blue feet!"

"Bingo!" cries Captain Turbot. "You've found it!"

To everyone's surprise, François takes off on his kitesurf board.

"Wait, François," says Captain Turbot. "You're going to scare the booby bird!"

But François calls back, "I will get the photo for you!"

François lands near the bird and gets out his camera.

"Say 'Le Cheese!'" shouts François. The booby bird flies straight at him.

"Mad booby bird!" cries François.

François falls off the cliff edge and clings on with one hand!

Skye quickly flies over. She lowers Captain Turbot down to François.

"Hang on, François," calls Captain Turbot. "Help is here!"

"Help, Horatio!" cries François. "This is a very angry booby bird."

The booby bird hops onto François's hand. He lets go of the cliff in fright and lands in the sea.

The PAW Patrol help François onto the boat and Captain Turbot turns to the booby bird.

"Hello, beautiful birdie," says Captain Turbot. "Can I take your picture please?"

The bird poses happily. CLICK!

Later, on the boat, François is shivering.

"Are you OK?" says Captain Turbot.

"I am," says François. "Thanks to you, Horatio. And the PAW Patrol."

Later at the park, Captain Turbot gives Ryder a present.

"I brought you this picture of the blue-footed booby bird to thank you," says Captain Turbot.

"Thanks!" says Ryder. "Whenever you're in trouble, just yelp for help!"